D1024689

This
Book Belongs
to...
Aiden Lynch

THE ENGLISH ROSES

FRIENDS FOR LIFE!

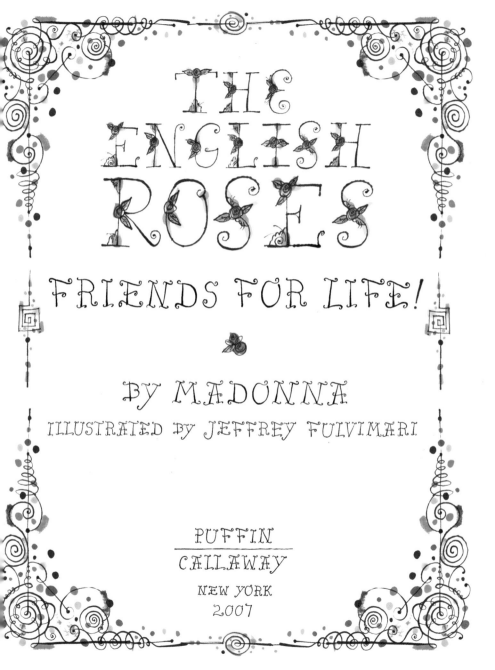

BY MADONNA

ILLUSTRATED BY JEFFREY FULVIMARI

PUFFIN

CALLAWAY

NEW YORK

2007

CALLAWAY ARTS & ENTERTAINMENT

19 FULTON STREET, FIFTH FLOOR, NEW YORK, NEW YORK 10038

PUFFIN BOOKS

Published by the Penguin Group
Penguin Young Readers Group, 345 Hudson Street, New York, New York 10014, U.S.A.
Penguin Group (Canada), 90 Eglinton Avenue East, Suite 700, Toronto, Ontario,
Canada M4P2Y3 (a division of Pearson Penguin Canada Inc.)

Penguin Books Ltd., Registered Offices: 80 Strand, London WC2R 0RL, England

First published in the United States of America by Callaway Arts & Entertainment and Puffin Books, 2007

1   3   5   7   9   10   8   6   4   2

First Edition

Produced by Callaway Arts & Entertainment
Nicholas Callaway, President and Publisher
Cathy Ferrara, Managing Editor and Production Director
Toshiya Masuda, Art Director • Nelson Gómez, Director of Digital Technology
Joya Rajadhyaksha, Editor • Amy Cloud, Editor
Ivan Wong, Jr. and José Rodríguez, Production
Kathryn Bradwell, Executive Assistant to the Publisher

Special thanks to Doug Whiteman and Mariann Donato.

Library of Congress Cataloging-in-Publication Data is available.

Puffin Books ISBN 978-0-14-241114-8

Printed in China

www.madonna.com   www.callaway.com   www.penguin.com/youngreaders

All of Madonna's proceeds from this book will be donated to
Raising Malawi (www.raisingmalawi.org), an orphan-care initiative.

TABLE OF CONTENTS

HELLO

We're the English Roses—Binah, Grace, Amy, Charlotte, and Nicole. We're best friends who do everything together.

On the last day of school last year, our awesome fifth-grade teacher, Miss Fluffernutter, suggested we make a book listing all of our favorite things, people, and memories. She told us that she and her friends made a similar book when they were our age, and she loves looking at it now. Well, we think anything Miss Fluffernutter does is the coolest, so all summer we passed this book around to one another and recorded everything—our biggest crushes, our favorite ice cream flavors, and especially our hopes and dreams for the future. We also included some special sections, like study tips, a British glossary, and a peek inside fashionista Amy's bag—even a postcard from foreign-exchange cutie Dominic de la Guardia!

We hope you have as much fun reading our book as we've had making it!

Cheers,

Binah Grace Amy
Charlotte Nicole

The Stars:
the English Roses

Binah
the serious one

Grace
the jock

Amy
the fashionista

Charlotte
the posh one

Nicole
the brainiac

Supporting Cast

Miss Fluffernutter
the coolest teacher ever

Fairy Godmother
the sassy one

Mr. Rossi
Binah's papa

**Dominic
de la Guardia**
the heartthrob

Bunny Love & Candy Darling
the dancing duo

Timmy Ferguson
the big brother

Terry Ferguson
the naughty brother

**Taffy & Tricky
Ferguson**
the twins

Mr. Ferguson
the fiddle-playing
father

The Queen
everyone's favorite monarch

{ Vital Statistics }

Full name: Binah Rossi

Nickname: B

Birthday: November 24

Astrological sign: Sagittarius

Birthplace: London

Eye color: Blue

Hair color: Blonde

Height: 4'9"

Family: Me and my papa — my mum died when I was very little.

Pet(s): None

BINAH

Who is your BFF? The English Roses: Nicole, Amy, Charlotte, and Grace.

Name one thing that you can do better than any of your friends.

Housework!

What is the best gift you ever received? Last year when Grace traveled around Europe with her family, she brought me back a bracelet with a charm from each country she had visited. It was so sweet of her to think of me throughout her trip.

When you grow up, what do you want to be?

A teacher.

You can't wait till the day you get to be a teacher, just like Miss Fluffernutter.

Worst habit: Giggling for no reason

What is one secret about you that only your closest friends know?

That I am color-blind.

What is the most embarrassing thing that ever happened to you? Last week I was running late and quickly rubbed on some lip balm before leaving the house. People were giving me funny looks on the street and I couldn't figure out why. It was only when I got to school that my friends told me I'd used a tinted balm — and smeared my entire mouth, not just my lips, bright pink!

go Binah!

13

 **BINAH**

Heroes: *My mum*

Person/People you'd like to meet: *I wish I could travel back in time to meet Queen Elizabeth the First.*

Celebrity crush: *Bono*

Real-life crush: *Dominic de la Guardia*

IM name: *Bee*

What nail polish shade are you wearing today?
I don't wear nail polish.

Are your ears pierced? *no*

If you had to choose, which do you think best describes your personal style?

a. Sporty   b. Funky   (c. Casual)   d. Classic   e. Dressy

Which best describes your personality?

a. Girly girl   b. Tomboy   (c. Studious)   d. Fashionable   e. Goofy

Favorite lip gloss flavor: *I don't wear lip gloss.*

Fashion icon: Hmmm...I'm not that into fashion. I love the way Charlotte dresses, though.

Favorite color: pale blue

If your shoes did the talking, what would they say about you?

That I wear them a lot!

Favorite book: Anne of Green Gables

How do you want to celebrate your next birthday?

A tea party with the English Roses.

What is your favorite thing in your room?

My doll

BINAH

even with all the work i have to do, i still make time for

after-school daydreaming

When you can't fall

asleep, what do you think about?

I try to remember what my mum was like.

Favorite way to spend a rainy afternoon: A trip to the

British Museum with my papa

Car you would like to drive someday: I'd love to drive a

Smart Car someday — they're so cute.

Three things you can't live without: The only thing I can't live

without is the doll my

mum gave me when

I was a baby.

eeek!

the "I'll-do-it-later" Monster

Which is your favorite subject at school, and which do you like least?

I love history, but I'm always so confused in computer class.

Whom do you sit next to at school? Charlotte.

Gym class is the only class where my clothes are the same as everyone else's.

What sports do you play?

Field hockey. I also run and swim.

Binah!

...ever the peacemaker

BINAH

Who is your favorite teacher? *Miss Fluffernutter*

What do you like to do after school? *Hang out with the English Roses before I go home to do chores.*

What's your favorite after-school snack? *chips*

Favorite food: *grilled cheese sandwiches*

The yummiest ice cream flavor: *butterscotch*

The yuckiest vegetable: *turnips*

Favorite pizza toppings: *I like plain cheese pizza.*

You can't leave home without *a barrette in my hair and a picture of my mum in my bag.*

my mum

What is your best physical feature?

I don't know... you'll have to ask my friends that.

What is your guilty pleasure?

long, hot bubble baths

What is your favorite movie?

Oliver Twist.

What is your pet peeve? spoiled brats

What doesn't come easily to you?

fussing over my looks

If you found 10 pounds on the street,

what would you do with the money?

Give it to my papa.

BINAH

How would you react if someone cheated off your work?

I'd be disappointed, but I wouldn't say anything.

What most often gets you in trouble?

Talking on the phone.

Favorite season: *Spring, when all the birds fly back and all the flowers are in bloom*

Do you speak any languages besides English?

A bit of French, and I'm planning to learn Spanish soon, too.

Where do you want to live when you grow up?

London.

If you were stranded on a desert island, which three things would you want to have with you? Why? Actually, I'd want four— Nicole, Amy, Charlotte, and Grace—because together we'd figure out a way to save ourselves.

What did you do over the summer? I went to visit my grandmother in Cornwall. We had the best time together!

Binah's Time-Saving Tips...

Since my mother died when I was very young, I've had to grow up a little bit faster than other girls my age. Running our household is my responsibility, and I've become something of an expert at doing things as efficiently as possible; that way, I can have even more time for fun things, like hanging out with the English Roses. Here are some tips that can help you manage your time more effectively, too.

PACK A LUNCH THE NIGHT BEFORE

Keep frantic mornings in check by making your lunch the night before. Put everything in a lunch sack and keep it in the refrigerator overnight. In the morning, don't forget to slip it into your schoolbag before you leave!

LAY OUT YOUR CLOTHES THE NIGHT BEFORE

Figure out what you want to wear the next day, and if possible, lay it out on a chair the night before so it's all ready to go. If you want to be really organized, pick out your outfits for the entire week and write them down so you don't forget!

KEEP A PLANNER

It may sound silly, but a calendar or planner that you can carry around with you is a big time- (and life-) saver! Write down all of your homework assignments, extracurricular activities, and plans with friends so you don't forget anything.

CLEAN OUT YOUR SCHOOLBAG ONCE A WEEK

A weekly dusting out of your schoolbag can really work wonders. Throw or file away old tests or papers that can be confusing and get in the way of more recent assignments.

GET A BULLETIN BOARD

Post mementos, keepsakes, photos, concert ticket stubs, and important fliers on a bulletin board in your room. It's a great way to cut down on paper clutter and to remind yourself of fun memories as well as exciting future events.

GRACE

{ Vital Statistics }

Full name: _Grace Harrison_

Nickname: _Gracie_

Birthday: _April 10_

Astrological sign: _Aries_

Birthplace: _Atlanta, Georgia_

Eye color: _Brown_   Hair color: _Black_

Height: _4' 7"_

Family: _Mom, Dad, and twin brothers, Matthew and Michael, 16 years old_

Pet(s): _I don't have any pets._

 **GRACE**

Who is your BFF? *Nicole, Amy, Charlotte, and Binah*

Name one thing that you can do better than any of your friends.

That's easy—play sports!

What is the best gift you ever received?

My friends chipped in and got me a subscription to Sports Illustrated magazine. I love reading about all kinds of sports.

When you grow up, what do you want to be?

I want to be a soccer star, but it's called football here in England.

You can't wait till the day you *are allowed to go to football games without my parents. It will be so cool to go with my friends!*

26

Worst habit: I bite my nails.

What is one secret about you that only your closest friends know?

I sometimes pretend I'm grown up and try on my mom's dresses.

What is the most embarrassing thing that ever happened to you?

It just happened the other day. My backpack was open, and I accidentally dropped it, spilling everything. There was stuff everywhere, including my sports bra. Everyone saw it and laughed! It was super-horrible!

Heroes: David Beckham and Mia Hamm

GRACE

Person/People you'd like to meet: Venus and Serena Williams. They're awesome!

Celebrity crush: David Beckham

Real-life crush: The boys

I know are lame. I don't like any of them.

IM name: GracieH

What nail polish shade are you wearing today?

I don't wear nail polish. Ever!

Are your ears pierced? No

If you had to choose, which do you think best describes your personal style?

(a. Sporty)   b. Funky   c. Casual   d. Classic   e. Dressy

Which best describes your personality?

a. Girly girl (b. Tomboy) c. Studious d. Fashionable e. Goofy

Favorite lip gloss flavor: Eww. I don't wear lip gloss!

Fashion icon: Maria Sharapova looks cool on and off the tennis court.

Favorite color: lavender

If your shoes did the talking, what would they say about you?

That girl can run!

How do you want to celebrate your next birthday? I would love to have a roller-skating party.

What is your favorite thing in your room?

My David Beckham poster. For sure!

29

GRACE

When you can't fall asleep, what do you think about?

I imagine playing the best game of my life and scoring the winning goal!

Favorite way to spend a rainy afternoon:

Having lunch with my best friends

Car you would like to drive someday:

Range Rover

Favorite book:

All of the Judy Moody books. They're so funny!

Three things you can't live without: 1. My poster of David Beckham, because he signed it

2. My favorite football

3. My best friends, Amy, Charlotte, Binah, and Nicole

Which is your favorite subject at school, and which do you like least?

Science is my favorite subject, because you get to learn about things all around you. Music is my least favorite, because we're practicing baby songs like "Edelweiss."

Whom do you sit next to at school?

This year, I sit next to Charlotte and a boy named Timothy.

Gym class is the best part of the day!

GRACE

What sports do you play?

I like all sports, but football is my favorite.

Who is your favorite teacher? Miss Fluffernutter

What do you like to do after school? If it's
nice out, I like to go to
the park with my friends.
If it isn't, I like to read.

What is your favorite after-school snack?

Red Vines.

Favorite food: French fries

The yummiest ice cream flavor:

Butterscotch Swirl

The yuckiest vegetable:

All vegetables are yucky! Brussels sprouts are the worst!

Favorite pizza toppings: pepperoni with extra cheese

You can't leave home without My sneakers or trainers, as they call them in London.

What is your best physical feature? My legs

What is your guilty pleasure? I love watching old dancing movies like Dirty Dancing. They're so romantic!

What is your favorite movie? Bend It Like Beckham

What is your pet peeve? I don't like it when people just assume that all athletes are dumb. We're not!

What doesn't come easily to you? Sitting still. I get bored unless I'm doing something.

GRACE

If you found 10 pounds on the street, what would you do with the money?

I would add it to my savings. I'm saving up for a ticket to the World Cup in South Africa in 2010.

How would you react if someone cheated off your work?

I would tease them mercilessly.

What most often gets you in trouble?

I leave my stuff all over the house and it makes my mom crazy!

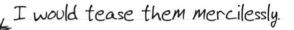

Favorite season: Autumn, because it's football season.

Do you speak any languages besides English?

No

Where do you want to live when you grow up?

In a house that's close to a park, so I can play football whenever I want.

If you were stranded on a desert island, which three things would you want to have with you? Why?

1. My sneakers.

2. My football.

3. A mobile phone, so I could call my friends and my family to pick me up!

What did you do over the summer?

Since I was born in Atlanta, Georgia, we have lots of relatives there. Every summer we spend two weeks with my cousins. It's really fun.

Grace's Glossary

When I first moved to London from Atlanta, Georgia, I was always confused at the way English people spoke. Here's my handy glossary translating Brit-speak to Ameri-speak!

JOLLY OLD ENGLAND	U.S.A.
biscuits	= cookies
brolly	= umbrella
brill	= brilliant
dust bin	= trash can
flat	= apartment
football	= soccer
knackered	= tired
knickers	= underwear
lift	= elevator
loo	= restroom
nosy Parker	= busybody
ring	= to call on the phone
rubbish	= trash
telly	= television
trainers	= sneakers
tube	= subway

My Saturday
by Grace

Can you translate the story below using my glossary?

When I woke up this morning I was so knackered I could hardly put on my knickers! Luckily, my fancy new trainers got me to the tube in half the time it would usually take. I hopped on and made it to my destination very quickly. While taking the lift to Nicole's grandmother's flat, I couldn't help jiggling my legs—the loo was calling my name! When I finally arrived, all of the English Roses were already there for our biscuit-making party. Unfortunately, since we were all glued to the telly, the biscuits burned in the oven! Sadly, we had to throw them in the dust bin with the other rubbish. I rang my mum to pick me up for football practice at 4 P.M. I scored a goal—brill!—but by the time practice was over, I was completely knackered once again!

A

is my
favorite
letter!

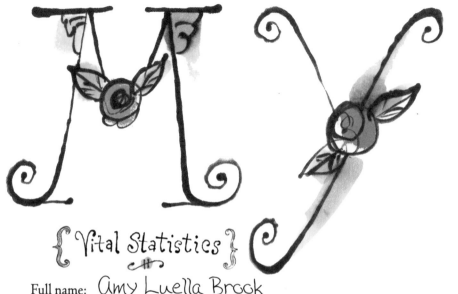

{ Vital Statistics }

Full name: Amy Luella Brook

Nickname: Carrots

Birthday: August 4

Astrological sign: Leo

Birthplace: London

Eye color: Green

Hair color: Red

Height: 4 feet 7 inches

Family: Dad, Mum and stepdad,
little sister, Chloe, and
a baby on the way

AMY

Who is your BFF?

Nicole, Charlotte, Grace, and Binah.

Name one thing that you can do better than any of your friends.

Accessorize.

What is the best gift you ever received?

For my tenth birthday, my mum
gave me her old Rolling
Stones concert tee that
she wore as a teenager.

When you grow up, what do you want to be?

fashion designer

You can't wait till the day you:

attend my first fashion show.

Worst habit: I crack my knuckles a lot.

40

What is one secret about you that only your closest friends know? I am terrified my father will get remarried and won't be able to spend much time with me.

What is the most embarrassing thing that ever happened to you?

My mum bought me a to-die-for dress to wear to a school dance, but I needed a bit of "help" filling out the top part. So, I used some wadded-up tissues. But while I was dancing up a storm, a few pieces of tissue fell out of the dress. My face turned as red as my hair!

Heroes: Coco Chanel! I just read an article about her; she founded the fashion label Chanel and is responsible for all of those fabulous little black dresses!

 AMY

Person/People you'd like to meet:

Stella McCartney

Celebrity crush: Orlando Bloom

Real-life crush: Ryan Hudson

IM name: KewlGrl82

What nail polish shade are you wearing today? Red Hot

Are your ears pierced? yep

If you had to choose, which do you think best describes your personal style?

a. Sporty   (b. Funky)   c. Casual   d. Classic   e. Dressy

Which best describes your personality?

a. Girly girl   b. Tomboy   c. Studious   d. Fashionable   (e. Goofy)

Favorite lip gloss flavor: Bubblegum

Fashion icon: Audrey Hepburn

Favorite color: Red

42

Fashion

If your shoes did the talking, what would they say about you?

That I have excellent taste.

How do you want to celebrate your next birthday?

Shopping spree with my best friends, and then all the bangers and mash we can eat!

What is your favorite thing in your room?

My old movie posters. I just love Audrey Hepburn!

When you can't fall asleep, what do you think about?

The fall fashion collections.

Favorite way to spend a rainy afternoon: Shopping

Car you would like to drive someday:

Union Jack Mini Cooper

amy Luella Brook Spring Collection...

AMY

Favorite book:

<u>Vogue Fashion</u>—I love all of the pictures!

Three things you can't live without: makeup kit, sketchbook, next month's fashion magazines

Which is your favorite subject at school, and which do you like least?

I love art class, especially when we get to sketch and paint. I HATE science—bugs and frogs are gross.

Whom do you sit next to at school?

Nicole

Gym class is okay if I can wear my designer gym clothes.

Sometimes a Rose's life can get VERY Heavy, dude...

What sports do you play? None—unless there are cute boys on the team.

Who is your favorite teacher?

Miss Fluffernutter

What do you like to do after school?

shop

What is your favorite after-school snack?

Cadbury Creme Eggs

Favorite food: Fish-and-chips

The yummiest ice cream flavor:

Mint Chocolate Chip.

The yuckiest vegetable: broccoli.

Favorite pizza toppings: ham and sausage

You can't leave home without nail polish.

What is your best physical feature?

my green eyes

What is your guilty pleasure?

Eavesdropping on my father's phone conversations when he's speaking to famous clients.

What is your favorite movie?

Breakfast at Tiffany's

What is your pet peeve? People who wear sweatpants in public!

What doesn't come easily to you?

Wearing the same outfit twice.

If you found 10 pounds on the street, what would you do with the money?

Buy a new lip gloss.

How would you react if someone cheated off your work?

I would ask my friends what I should do.

What most often gets you in trouble?

Talking too much in class.

Favorite season: Fall because of the fashion!

47

AMY

Do you speak any languages besides English? nope

Where do you want to live when you grow up? Milan

If you were stranded on a desert island, which three things would you want

to have with you? Why?

1. my super-deluxe portable makeup kit
(instant camouflage!)

2. my sketchbook (I'm sure there's lots of
fashion inspiration on desert islands.)

48

3. my mum's killer pointy Jimmy Choo boots that almost fit me (to ward off predators)

What did you do over the summer?

I went with my mum to Mozambique.

Inside Amy's Bag:

You can definitely tell a lot about a girl by looking inside...

LUNCH MONEY
Just in case the cafeteria is serving anything edible

HAIR PRODUCTS
To keep my curls in check

LIP GLOSS
To keep my lips soft (just in case Ryan Hudson wants to kiss me)

FASHION MAGAZINES
So I'm in the know on the latest trends

SKETCHBOOK
You never know when fashion inspiration will strike!

PENCILS
'Cause I have to do schoolwork sometimes

CHOCOLATES
For sweet-tooth emergencies

CHAR

{ Vital Statistics }

Full name: Charlotte Ginsberg

Nickname: Charlie

Birthday: September 4

Astrological sign: Virgo

Birthplace: London

Eye color: Brown   Hair color: Black

Height: 5'

Family: Parents, Nigel and Olivia; older sister, Emma; younger brother, Patrick

Pet(s): A pony named Posie

CHARLOTTE

Who is your BFF? The English Roses and my diary.

Name one thing that you can do better than any of your friends.

Ride a horse.

What is the best gift you ever received? Charlotte

A designer handbag.

When you grow up, what do you want to be?

A socialite, like my mum.

You can't wait till the day you can go

to a debutante ball.

Worst habit:

doing my homework at the last minute.

What is one secret about you that only your closest friends know?

That I'm very self-conscious
about dancing.

What is the most embarrassing thing that ever happened to you?

Once I was daydreaming when a new teacher asked our names in class. When it was my turn to answer, I said my crush's name by mistake!

Heroes: Hilary Duff

Person/People you'd like to meet: Daniel Radcliffe

Celebrity crush: Daniel Radcliffe

Real-life crush: William Worthington

IM name: Charlotte

What nail polish shade are you wearing today?

I have a French manicure.

# CHARLOTTE

Are your ears pierced? _no_

If you had to choose, which do you think best describes your personal style?

    a. Sporty   b. Funky   c. Casual   (d. Classic)   e. Dressy

Which best describes your personality?

    (a. Girly girl)   b. Tomboy   c. Studious   d. Fashionable e. Goofy

Favorite lip gloss flavor: _Seashell, by Chanel_

Fashion icon: _my mother_

Favorite color: _pink_

If your shoes did the talking, what would they say about you?

That I am very stylish and posh.

How do you want to celebrate your next birthday?

High tea at Claridge's with the English Roses, and then shopping at Harrods.

What is your favorite thing in your room? My walk-in closet

When you can't fall asleep, what do you

think about? Riding Posie in the

Olympics.

Favorite way to spend a rainy afternoon:

shopping

Car you would like to drive someday:

a pink Aston Martin

Favorite book: The Famous

Five series

Three things you can't live without: blow-dryer, lip gloss,

pink Prada pen case

Which is your favorite subject at school, and which do you like least?

History is brill, but I hate biology.

CHARLOTTE

Whom do you sit next to at school?

Binah and Grace.

Gym class is AWFUL— I always break my nails!

What sports do you play?

None, but I love riding horses.

Who is your favorite teacher?

Miss Fluffernutter

What do you like to do after school?

shop

What is your favorite after-school snack?

tea with scones and clotted cream

Favorite food: sushi

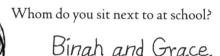

The yummiest ice cream flavor: pistachio

The yuckiest vegetable: cabbage

Favorite pizza toppings: artichokes

You can't leave home without splashing on some Jean Paul Gaultier perfume.

What is your best physical feature? my hair

What is your guilty pleasure?

Eating Gushers candy in bed at night.

CHARLOTTE

What is your favorite movie? That's easy—The Princess Diaries.

What is your pet peeve? sloppiness

What doesn't come easily to you? ignoring gossip

If you found 10 pounds on the street, what would you do with the money? Not much! Oh well, buy some Gushers, I guess.

How would you react if someone cheated off your work? I'd be proud that they thought I was so smart!

What most often gets you in trouble? Spending my allowance too quickly.

Favorite season: Autumn

Do you speak any languages besides English? Yes, French.

Where do you want to live when you grow up? Paris

If you were stranded on a desert island, which three things would

you want to have with you? Why?

A hairbrush, a mirror, and some lip gloss, so that I look good when I'm rescued!

What did you do over the summer?

My family went to our villa in the south of France, where we go every year.

Charlotte's Etiquette 101

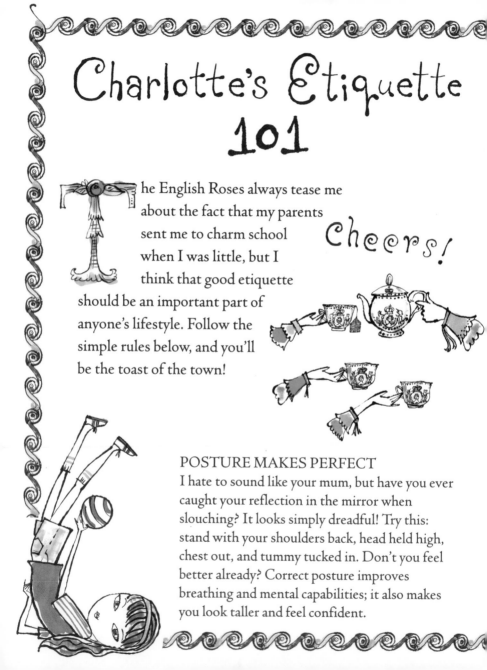

The English Roses always tease me about the fact that my parents sent me to charm school when I was little, but I think that good etiquette should be an important part of anyone's lifestyle. Follow the simple rules below, and you'll be the toast of the town!

Cheers!

POSTURE MAKES PERFECT

I hate to sound like your mum, but have you ever caught your reflection in the mirror when slouching? It looks simply dreadful! Try this: stand with your shoulders back, head held high, chest out, and tummy tucked in. Don't you feel better already? Correct posture improves breathing and mental capabilities; it also makes you look taller and feel confident.

BORROWING BASICS
The English Roses love to borrow one another's clothes—it's like having five times the wardrobe! However, whenever you borrow anything from a friend—be it a dress or a DVD—it's important to return it in the same condition as it was when you received it. In the case of the English Roses, we always wash, press, and neatly fold the clothing we borrow from one another.

MEALTIME MATTERS
Good table manners are essential in making a positive impression. Always chew with your mouth closed, and swallow your food before speaking. Place a napkin on your lap to catch any food spills, and be sure to ask fellow diners to pass dishes not within your reach. And please don't pick food from your teeth at the table—wait until after the meal to pick in private. Bon appétit!

SMILE—IT'S CONTAGIOUS!
It's amazing what a simple smile can do to brighten up someone else's day—and your own! The act of smiling makes your brain produce endorphins, substances that give you a natural sense of peace and well-being. Just another reason to flash your pearly whites more often.

COLE

{ Vital Statistics }

Full name: Nicole Sophie Rissman

Nickname: Nikki

Birthday: July 14

Astrological sign: Cancer

Birthplace: Paris, France

Eye color: Blue   Hair color: Dirty blonde

Height: 4' 9"

Family: Mum and Daddy

Pet(s): The cutest, smartest Jack

Russell terrier in the whole world, Aston

 # NICOLE

Who is your BFF? Charlotte, Grace, Amy, and Binah.

Name one thing that you can do better than any of your friends.

Actually, there are two: writing and dancing.

What is the best gift you ever received? My autographed Harry Potter boxed set.

When you grow up, what do you want to be?

A writer.

You can't wait till the day you publish my first book.

Worst habit: I bite my nails and chew my pencils.

What is one secret about you that only your closest friends know? I'm always afraid that my daddy will make us move again.

What is the most embarrassing thing that ever happened to you? I was swimming with a friend and this way-cute guy swam over to us. We started chatting and splashing around. At one point, I dove underwater, but when I came back up he gave me a funny look and quickly swam away. I couldn't figure out what was wrong. Later I realized I had had a huge gob of snot hanging out of my nose. I wanted to die.

NICOLE

Heroes: My nana, Hazel Rissman

Person/People you'd like to meet: J.K. Rowling

Celebrity crush: Joel Madden

Real-life crush: Brent Robertson, the cutest boy in school

IM name: TruBluNik14

What nail polish shade are you wearing today? Glum Plum

Are your ears pierced? Of course—twice.

If you had to choose, which do you think best describes your personal style?

a. Sporty   b. Funky   c. Casual   d. Classic   e. Dressy

Which best describes your personality?

in-between

a. Girly girl b. Tomboy c. Studious   d. Fashionable e. Goofy

Favorite lip gloss flavor: Dr. Pepper

Fashion icon: Avril Lavigne

Favorite color: deeeep navy blue

If your shoes did the talking, what would they say about you?

That I should stop writing on them (I doodle on my sneakers).

How do you want to celebrate your next birthday?

A dance party that I DJ myself, with my bestest friends (and Joel Madden, LOL!).

 NICOLE

What is your favorite thing in your room? My magic eight ball that predicts the future.

When you can't fall asleep, what do you think about? I imagine life when I'm older, living on my own as a famous writer in New York.

Favorite way to spend a rainy afternoon: reading in my room

Car you would like to drive someday: a navy blue Vespa scooter with matching helmet

Favorite book: Harriet the Spy

Three things you can't live without: CDs, the purple scarf I knit myself, my computer

Which is your favorite subject at school, and which do you like least?

Favorite: writing. Least: a tie between math and gym.

Whom do you sit next to at school?

Amy

Gym class is a total waste of my time.

What sports do you play? As if! None.

Who is your favorite teacher?

Miss Fluffernutter

What do you like to do after school?

read, go online, listen to music, hang out with my friends

What's your favorite after-school snack? chips and spicy salsa

NICOLE

I'M NICOLE

Favorite food: Indian

The yummiest ice cream flavor: dairy = double ick. But I do like chocolate tofutti.

The yuckiest vegetable: cauliflower = triple ick!

Favorite pizza toppings: I will only eat pizza that has green peppers, mushrooms, and no cheese.

You can't leave home without lip gloss and my iPod.

What is your best physical feature? I don't have one.

What is your guilty pleasure? Watching Little Rascals episodes and Shirley Temple movies.

What is your favorite movie? The Horse Whisperer.

What is your pet peeve? Smart girls who act dumb to impress boys.

What doesn't come easily to you? laughing

If you found 10 pounds on the street, what would you do with the money? Buy a CD.

How would you react if someone cheated off your work? I'd poke their eyes out with a pencil.

What most often gets you in trouble? My moodiness.

Favorite season: Winter

Do you speak any languages besides English? Je parle francais. (I speak French.)

 **NICOLE**

Where do you want to live when you grow up? New York

If you were stranded on a desert island, which three things would you want

to have with you? Why? My iPod, because I can't

live without music; a notebook, so I could write about being stranded on an island; the lucky pen my nana gave me, because I can't write without it.

What did you do over the summer?

I went to New York for a month with my daddy and mum.

Nicole's Study Tips

My friends often refer to me as the brains in the group, but the truth is that I'm no more brainy than they are—I've just developed good study habits. Try these out. They're sure to work for you, too.

DON'T PROCRASTINATE

Do your homework as soon as you get home—after a yummy snack, of course. That way you'll have the rest of the evening to chat on the phone, watch the telly, or do any old thing you want to do.

USE FLASH CARDS

I know it sounds babyish, but it really helps to write key points on flash cards for easy reference or last-minute cramming.

DO PRACTICE TESTS

Ask your teacher or older brothers and sisters for tests from previous years. This will give you an idea of what to expect and, if you're in luck, some of the questions may even be repeated.

PLAY SOME MUSIC

(Softly, though, and in the background.) Unlike the TV, which is a huge distraction, I always find that music helps me focus when I'm doing homework. At first my parents thought I was just goofing off—as if!

TAKE BREAKS

You won't get anything done if you're tired, so tear yourself away from the computer before your eyes turn googly, and stop writing before your hand cramps up.

Hola, Señorita!

Greetings from Alájar! It's a little strange for me to be back in Spain after such a long time. I keep using English words in school! I'm really happy to be with my mamá and papá again, though, and to be eating homemade paella and frittatas instead of kidney pie. I don't miss English food, but I do miss the English Roses, especially you — I hope you'll come and visit me soon. In the meanwhile, tell me what everyone has been up to. Is Grace on the football team again this year? And is Nicole still planning to write a song for the talent competition? What about Amy and Charlotte? I can't wait to hear all the news.

Adiós and XO,

Dominic

To:

Binah Rossi

12 Tulip Square

London WS7 52J

United Kingdom

horrible
drawing
of someone

Paste or draw your image here

Vital Statistics

writen when I was 5

Full name: Aiden N

Nickname: ~~Aide~~ Ai Ai

Birthday: jenoRe 19

Astrological sign: Got

Birthplace: jenoReia

Eye color: ~~Yeloy~~ brown

Hair color: BRAwn

Height: ~~mmi~~ ? 4 feet

Family: JHnL OGas Chris

Pet(s): Chicehs

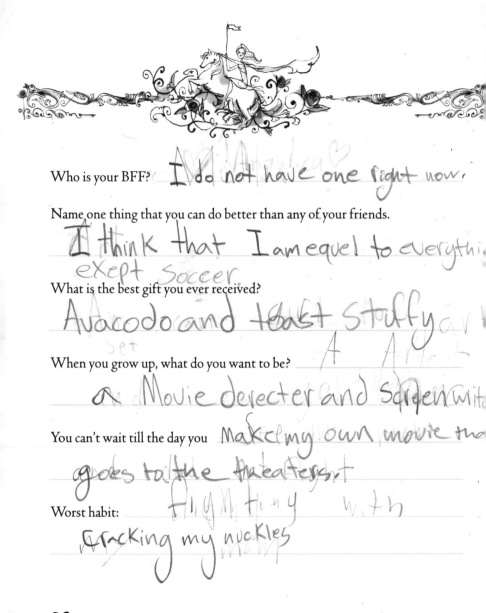

Who is your BFF? I do not have one right now.

Name one thing that you can do better than any of your friends.
I think that I am equel to everythi
exept soccer.

What is the best gift you ever received?
Avacodo and toast stuffy art
set

When you grow up, what do you want to be?
a Movie derecter and sargen with

You can't wait till the day you Make my own movie tha
goes to the theatersit

Worst habit: fighting with
Cracking my nuckles

What is one secret about you that only your closest friends know?

I am I do not kNOW

What is the most embarrassing thing that ever happened to you?

I do NOT Know

Heroes: George Lucos, and my family

Person/People you'd like to meet: George Lucos

Celebrity crush: Nobody

Real-life crush: Nobody

IM name: Do not Know what that means, so I do not have one.

What nail polish shade are you wearing today? I do not where nail polish unless for special acations

Are your ears pierced? yes

If you had to choose, which do you think best describes your personal style?

Between

a. Sporty   b. Funky   c. Casual   d. Classic   e. Dressy

Which best describes your personality?

a. Girly girl   b. Tomboy   c. Studious   d. Fashionable   e. Goofy

Favorite lip gloss flavor: I do not wear Lip gloss (or anything like it)

Fashion icon: I do not pay attention to fashin.

Favorite color: Rainbow

If your shoes did the talking, what would they say about you?

That I do not Know, They don't talk.

How do you want to celebrate your next birthday?

Climbing and Cooking

What is your favorite thing in your room? My butterfly that my sister gave me.

When you can't fall asleep, what do you think about?

I make up Stories in my head.

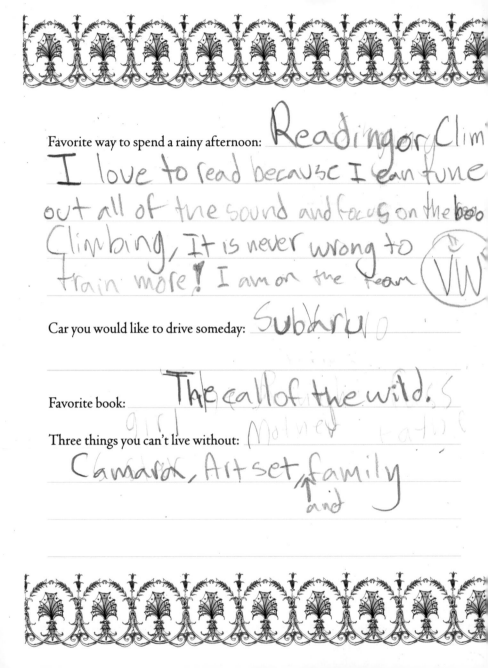

Favorite way to spend a rainy afternoon: Reading or Clim

I love to read because I can tune out all of the sound and focus on the boo Climbing, It is never wrong to train more! I am on the team VW

Car you would like to drive someday: Subaru

Favorite book: The call of the wild.

Three things you can't live without: girl Mother fath
Camaro, Art set, family and

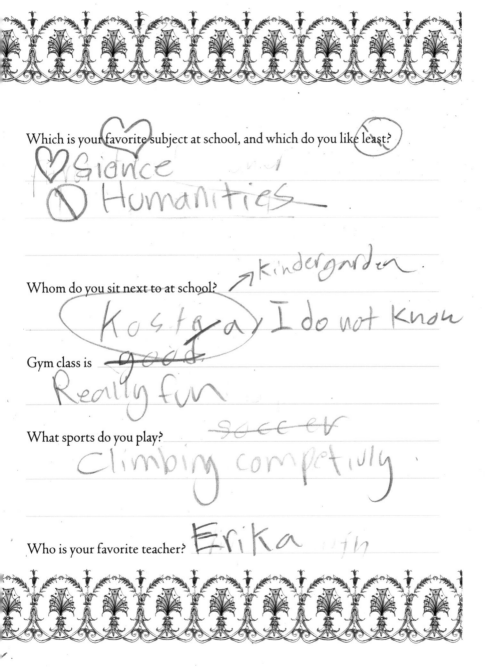

Which is your favorite subject at school, and which do you like least?

♡ Sicnce

Ⓝ Humanities

Whom do you sit next to at school? → kindergarden

Kostga I do not know

Gym class is ~~good~~

Really fun

What sports do you play? ~~soccer~~

Climbing competivly

Who is your favorite teacher? Erika

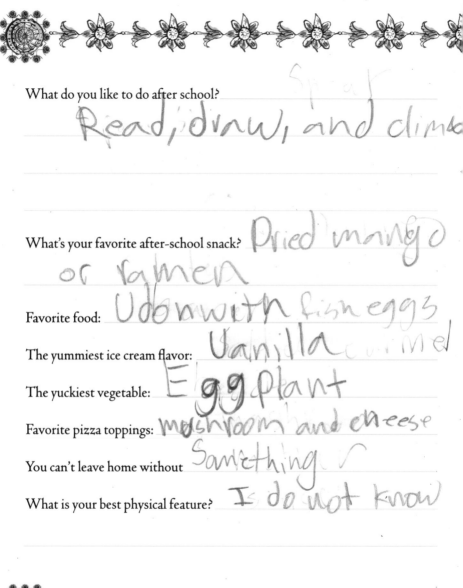

What do you like to do after school? Spiral

Read, draw, and climb

What's your favorite after-school snack? Dried mango
or ramen

Favorite food: Udon with fish eggs

The yummiest ice cream flavor: Vanilla caramel

The yuckiest vegetable: Eggplant

Favorite pizza toppings: mushroom and cheese

You can't leave home without Something

What is your best physical feature? I do not know

What is your guilty pleasure? ~~Duke~~

I do not know

What is your favorite movie? ? ~~movies~~

What is your pet peeve? People with no headphones

What doesn't come easily to you? ~~Math~~

Not hurrying and not getting frustrated when people don't

If you found 10 dollars on the street, what would you do with the money?

Put $2 in my collage savings and $4 in my sisters and $4 in my parents retirment

How would you react if someone cheated off your work?

I would get mad and leave an anonymus note to the teacher

What most often gets you in trouble?

lieing about stuff.

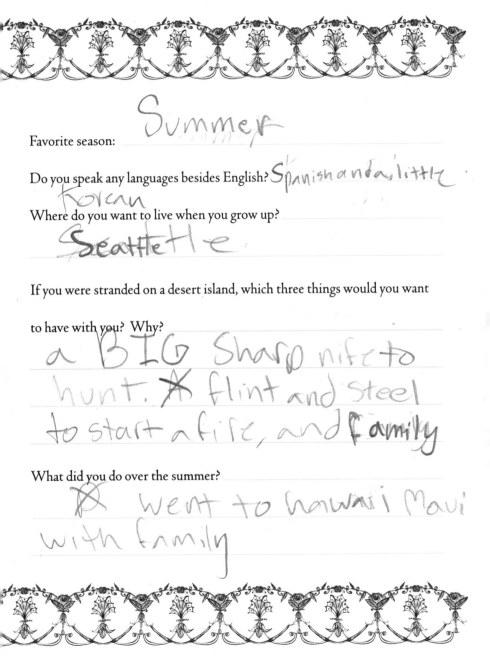

Favorite season: _Summer_

Do you speak any languages besides English? _Spanish and a little_
Korean

Where do you want to live when you grow up? _____

Seattle He

If you were stranded on a desert island, which three things would you want

to have with you? Why?

a BIG Sharp nife to
hunt. ✗ flint and steel
to start a fise, and family

What did you do over the summer?

✗ went to hawaii Maui
with family

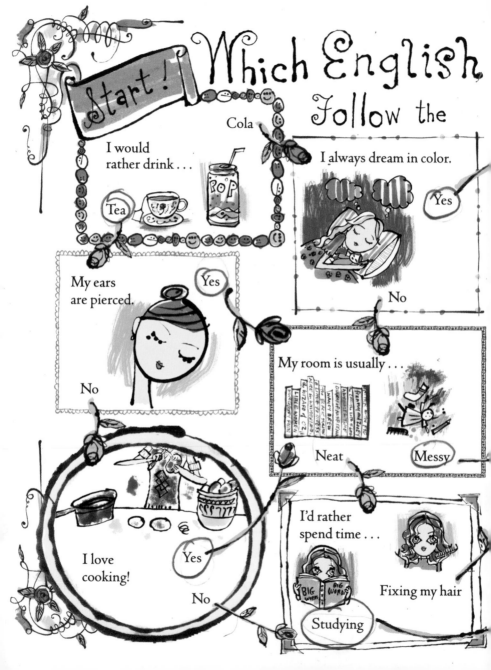

Start!

Which English

Follow the

Cola

I would rather drink . . .

Tea

I always dream in color.

Yes

No

My ears are pierced.

Yes

No

My room is usually . . .

Neat

Messy

I love cooking!

Yes

No

I'd rather spend time . . .

Fixing my hair

Studying

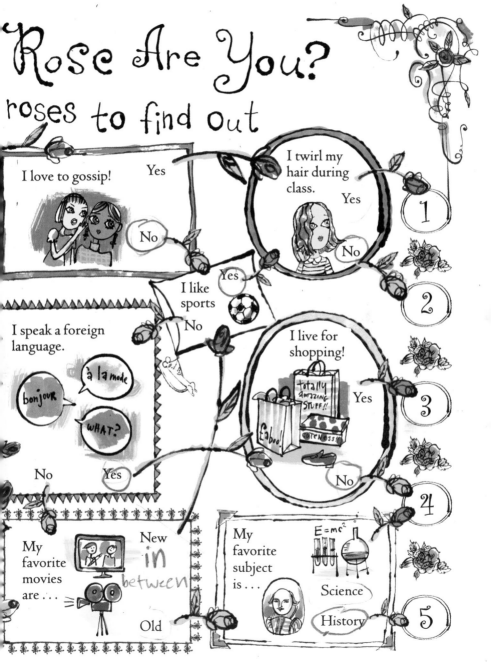

YOU ARE SOOO...

1

AMY:
Funky and forever unique, your flair for fashion has won you admirers near and far. You're never afraid to speak your mind, which gets you in trouble sometimes; but your friends appreciate your pure heart and fierce loyalty.

2

CHARLOTTE:
Prim and proper through and through, your perfect day involves sipping tea and shopping with your mum. Though others may think you're all about appearance, on the inside you're a very sensitive, caring person.

3 BINAH:

Soft-spoken and as gentle as a bird, you'd rather spend an evening reading about Queen Elizabeth than poring over fashion magazines. Your innate wisdom makes you the go-to girl for friends with problems.

4 NICOLE:

Others may say you're dark and moody, but on the inside you're all mushy. You brood around town with your iPod, scribbling in notebooks and daydreaming about intellectual pursuits; but you're never too busy to gossip with your friends.

5 GRACE:

You'd rather spend a day on the soccer field than shop, and though you hate to admit it, boys who can score a goal make your day. You may have a tough exterior, but on the inside you have a soft spot for romantic movies. Your friends always appreciate how much you try to protect them.

MADONNA RITCHIE was born in Bay City, Michigan, and now lives in London and Los Angeles with her husband, movie director Guy Ritchie, and her children, Lola, Rocco, and David. She has recorded 17 albums and appeared in 18 movies. This is the first in her series of chapter books. She has also written six picture books for children, starting with the international bestseller *The English Roses*, which was released in 40 languages and more than 100 countries.

ALSO BY MADONNA:

The English Roses
Mr. Peabody's Apples
Yakov and the Seven Thieves
The Adventures of Abdi
Lotsa de Casha
The English Roses: Too Good To Be True

JEFFREY FULVIMARI was born in Akron, Ohio. He started coloring when he was two, and has never stopped. Soon after graduating from The Cooper Union in New York City, he began drawing for magazines and television commercials around the globe. He currently lives in a log cabin in upstate New York, and is happiest when surrounded by stacks of paper and magic markers.

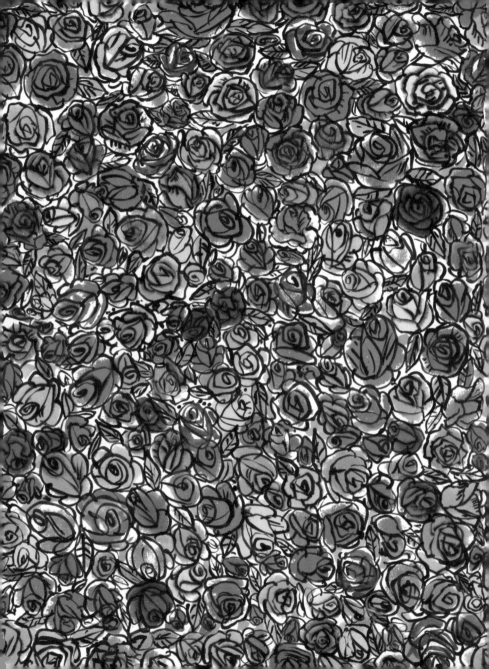